Library of Congress Cataloging in Publication Data

Andersen, H.C. (Hans Christian), 1805–1875.
The little mermaid.

Translation of: Lille havfrue.
Summary: A little sea princess, longing to be human,
trades her mermaid's tail for legs, hoping to win a
prince's love and earn an immortal soul for herself.
1. Children's stories, Danish. [1. Fairy tales.
2. Mermaids–Fiction] I. Iwasaki, Chihiro, 1918–1974,
ill. II. Title.
PZ8.A542Lit 1984b   [E]   84–9490
ISBN 0-907234-59-3

Illustrations copyright © 1967 by Chihiro Iwasaki.
English edition rights arranged by Kurita-Bando Literary Agency.
English text copyright © 1984 Neugebauer Press USA Inc.
Published in USA by Picture Book Studio USA,
an imprint of Neugebauer Press USA Inc.,
distributed by Alphabet Press, Natick, MA.
Distributed in Canada by Vanwell Publishing, St.Catharines.
All rights reserved.
Printed in Austria.

Ask your bookseller for these other Picture Book Studio books
by Hans Christian Andersen:
THE RED SHOES illustrated by Chihiro Iwasaki
THE NIGHTINGALE illustrated by Lisbeth Zwerger
THE SWINEHERD illustrated by Lisbeth Zwerger
THUMBELINE illustrated by Lisbeth Zwerger

The Little Mermaid

From the Story by
Hans Christian Andersen
illustrated by Chihiro Iwasaki
adapted by Anthea Bell

PICTURE BOOK STUDIO USA

Far out at sea the water is clear, and as blue as cornflowers. But it is very deep, so deep that no ship's anchor could ever reach the bottom. Mermaids and mermen live down there, and the Mer King has his palace on the seabed, where wonderful plants and trees grow, swaying gracefully with the movement of the water. Fish swim through their branches, just as birds fly through the branches of trees up on land. The palace itself is built of coral, its windows are all clear amber, and its roof is made of shells that open and close to show the shining pearls they hold.

The Mer King's wife had been dead for many years, and his old mother kept house for him and looked after his six children, the little mermaid princesses.

The youngest mermaid was the prettiest of them all.
She had skin like rose petals, and deep blue eyes.
But like her sisters, she had no feet; her body ended in a fish's tail instead.
The little mermaids played in the palace or the palace garden all day long,
or listened to their grandmother's wonderful stories of the world
above the waves.
They would not be allowed to go up and see it for themselves
until they reached the age of fifteen.

The youngest mermaid used to sit and dream of the sun. On calm days you could see it far away above the sea, like a purple flower streaming with light, and all the flowers the little mermaid grew in her garden were red as roses, to remind her of it. How she envied her elder sisters, as each in turn celebrated her fifteenth birthday and went up above the waves to sit on the rocks, and see what the rest of the world was really like! They all came back with tales of their own to tell.

At last her own fifteenth birthday came. Her grandmother gave her a heavy wreath of white lilies and pearls to wear, and she swam up and up through the water. She came out just at sunset, when the clouds were still glowing. The first thing she saw was a great ship, bright with lights, with many fine people on board, among them a handsome young prince. It was his birthday, and they were celebrating it with fireworks and music and dancing.

But soon a storm came up and drove the ship away. Enchanted by the handsome prince, the little mermaid followed. All the while, the waves rose high, the dark clouds gathered, and the lightning flashed.

The ship's timbers creaked, the mainmast snapped, and the ship heeled over as water rushed into her hold. Only then did the little mermaid understand that the people on board were in danger. As the ship sank, she saw the young prince fall into the sea, and at first she was pleased to think that he was coming down to her own country. Then she remembered that he could not live under water, and she made up her mind to save his life. She swam through the drifting spars and timbers of the wrecked ship, diving through the waves until at last she found him. He was exhausted and near dying, but the little mermaid held his head above water as the waves drove them on, until she saw land ahead at last. She left the prince on shore in a little bay, hid herself behind some rocks in the sea, and waited to see what would happen.

The land they had reached was very lovely, with high mountains, green forests, and a great white building near by, surrounded by a garden of orange and lemon trees and palms. A bell rang inside this building, and several young girls came out. One of them ran down to the sea shore. Finding the poor prince there, she quickly went to fetch help. When he revived, and saw the beautiful girl, he instantly fell in love with her, just as the little mermaid had fallen in love with him.

As for the little mermaid herself, watching all the time, she realized that he did not even know she was the one who had rescued him. He was carried away into the white building, and she swam home to her father's palace, very sad and sorrowful.

She grew sadder still as time went on, pining for the young prince.
She used to sit among the plants and fishes in her Mer King's garden and
think of him. At last she told her sisters of her sorrow. One of them knew
where the prince's own country lay, and they took her to his palace by the sea.
After that, she often swam there just to set eyes on him, although he knew
nothing at all about her.

"Tell me more about human beings," she said to her grandmother.
"Their earthly lives are shorter than ours, for we live three hundred years,"
said the old lady. "But when we die we are gone for ever, like foam on the sea,
while humans have immortal souls and rise to the stars in the sky after death."
"Can't a mermaid get an immortal soul?" the little mermaid asked.
"Not unless a man falls in love with her and marries her—but that can never be.
Humans think our pretty tails ugly, and prefer their own clumsy legs.
So cheer up, my dear, and enjoy your three hundred years of life!"

However, the little mermaid could not forget her prince. In her despair and her longing to be his wife and win an immortal soul, she went to ask the old Witch of the Sea for help.

"Yes, I can help you," said the Witch of the Sea, where she sat with the sea serpents coiling all around her. "I can give you a magic drink that will change your tail to a pair of legs. But every time you take a step, it will hurt like sharp knives cutting your feet. And if you do not win your prince's love, and he marries someone else, you will die the morning after his wedding. Nor will you be able to speak to him, or sing in your sweet voice, because I must cut out your tongue as my payment. Do you agree to all this?"

"Yes," said the little mermaid bravely, thinking of her prince and her soul.

So the Witch of the Sea cut out her little tongue and gave her the magic drink.

The little mermaid swam away. Her heart was nearly breaking at the thought of leaving her sisters for ever, but she went on, up and up through the deep blue sea. She reached the prince's palace by the sea before sunrise, and sat on its marble steps to drink her magic potion. As she drank, a terrible pain like a sword stroke shot through her. She fainted away. When she came back to her senses, she still felt the pain, but the sun had risen, and there stood the prince in front of her. Her tail had disappeared, and she had a pretty pair of legs instead. She had no clothes, so she wound her long hair around herself instead.

"Who are you, pretty child?" asked the prince. But she could not tell him, for she was dumb. So he took her into the palace, where they gave her beautiful silk and muslin dresses to wear. She longed to sing for the prince, but of course she could not, so she danced instead, with wonderful grace, in spite of the sharp pain it gave her. The prince made a kind of pet of her, and let her sleep on a velvet cushion outside his own door.

The prince used to take her out riding in the woods with him, among the green leaves. He became very fond of the dumb girl, although it never entered his head to ask her to marry him. She sadly realized that she would not get an immortal soul, and instead she must die and turn to sea foam on the morning after his wedding.

He told her that she reminded him of a lovely girl he had once seen, when he was washed up on a foreign shore, and this beautiful girl had saved his life.

"And I love none but her!" he said. "However, my parents know of a certain princess they want me to marry. I must go and look at her, but that is all I'll do! They can't force me to make her my bride. Why, you pretty, speechless child, I'd rather marry you, because you remind me of my true love!"

For a little while after that, she dared to dream again of becoming
his wife and winning an immortal soul.
The time came when the prince must set sail for the distant land
where the princess lived, and he took the little mermaid along with him.

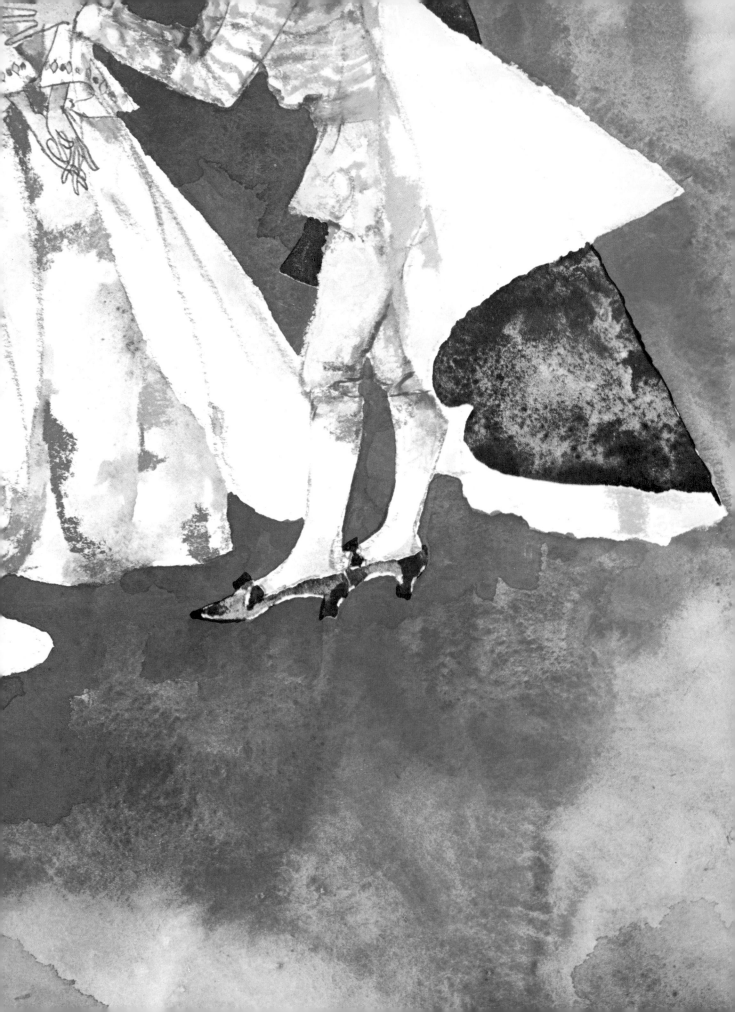

When the ship reached land, all the church bells in the foreign king's city were ringing. The princess herself arrived—and lo and behold, when the prince saw her, he recognized the girl he loved! She had been sent away to be brought up in the white building, a sacred temple. "It is you!" he cried. "You saved me from the sea! Oh, how happy I am!" he said, turning to the little mermaid. "And I know you are so fond of me that you will be happy for me too!"

The little mermaid kissed his hand, but she felt her heart would break.

The church bells rang for the wedding of the prince and princess. The little mermaid was bridesmaid, dressed all in silk and gold, and she carried the bride's train. But she did not hear the music or see the marriage ceremony. She was thinking of her own approaching death, and all that she had lost.

That very night the prince and his bride went on board the ship, and the little mermaid was with them. There was a magnificent tent on board where the newly married couple were to sleep.

It grew dark, lamps were lit, and the sailors danced on deck. The little mermaid danced too, more beautifully than ever before, though it hurt like walking on sharp knife blades. She knew this was the last night she would ever see the prince, who never guessed how she loved him, or knew what she had done for him.

The prince and his bride went into their tent, and the little mermaid stood by the ship's rail, waiting for the first light of dawn, which would kill her as the sun rose.

Then her sisters came up from the waves.

"We have been to the Witch of the Sea!" they said. "You need not die! She gave us this knife to help you. Thrust it into the prince's heart before sunrise. His blood will splash on your feet, changing them back into a fish's tail again, and you can come down to us in the water and live out your three hundred years. Hurry—either you or he must die before the sun rises!" And they sank back down into the sea.

So the little mermaid drew back the hangings around the tent, and saw the prince and princess sleeping there, clasped in one another's arms.
She kissed the prince's forehead, and looked at the sky, where the first light of dawn was showing. She looked at the knife in her hand, and back at the prince once more. He was murmuring his wife's name in his dreams. The knife shook in the little mermaid's hand, but she flung it out to sea. Where it fell, the water shone red like drops of blood. Then she flung herself into the sea too, and she felt that she was dissolving into foam.

But as the sun rose, she found she was not dead after all. She felt herself rising up and up into the air, which was full of beautiful, translucent shapes, murmuring musically in tones no mortal ear could hear.

"Who are you?" she asked in wonder, and found that she had a voice and an airy form like theirs.

"The children of the air!" they said. "You were a mermaid, with no immortal soul unless you could win one by gaining a human's love. We have no souls either, but we may gain them for ourselves by doing good. We are on our way to the hot countries now, to ease the sick by spreading cool breezes, sweet scents, and healing. And when we have done all the good we can for three hundred years, we will get immortal souls. Poor little mermaid! You have tried to do good too, and you have suffered, so now you are to join us, and you can earn your own soul."

Then the little mermaid lifted her arms to the sun she had always loved so much. She looked down, and saw the ship, with the prince and his princess gazing sadly at the sea as if they guessed she had thrown herself into it. She was invisible to them as she kissed the princess and smiled at the prince, and then she went sailing up to the rosy clouds with the children of the air.

"And in three hundred years," they whispered to her, "we will fly on and on and into the Kingdom of Heaven!"

PRESENTED TO

THE

SASSARINI LIBRARY

in honor of

the Library's 23rd Birthday

on

3/17/94

by

Jason Breau

S.V. Board of Education member
Friend of the Sassarini Library

Macmillan Publishing Company
866 Third Avenue
New York, NY 10022

Collier Macmillan Canada, Inc.
1200 Eglinton Avenue East
Suite 200
Don Mills, Ontario M3C 3N1

First published by Macmillan Children's Books, London
First American edition
Printed in Great Britain

1 2 3 4 5 6 7 8 9 10

Library of Congress CIP Data is available: LC 90-6363

ISBN 0-02-700251-9